William Work-a

CW00840491

Irene Howat

For Sandra and May

Christian Focus Publications

Mr William Work-a-lot had a son called James.
James had a pet hamster.

The hamster's name was Stuff
because he sometimes stuffed
so much food into
his cheeks that he
couldn't get through
his tunnel.

'Will you help me build my model plane tonight?'
James asked his dad at breakfast one morning.

Mr Work-a-lot looked at his big important diary. 'Sorry,
Son,' he said. 'I'm working late. I've got to work hard
to pay for all your toys.'

James took Stuff out of his cage and made a trail of sunflower seeds for him to follow and eat.

'I'd rather have Dad than all my toys,' he told the hamster.

'Will you read me a story?' James asked his dad.

Mr Work-a-lot looked at his big important diary. 'Sorry, Son,' he said. 'I am going to meet a customer tonight. I have to work hard to pay for our holidays.'

James took Stuff out of his cage. He let him run up inside his right shirt sleeve and down inside his left shirt sleeve.

'I'd rather have Dad than all our holidays,' he told the hamster.

'Will you play football with me tonight?' James asked his dad the next day. It was Friday, Mr Work-a-lot's busiest day.

He looked in his big important diary. 'Sorry, Son,' he said. 'I've to go to a meeting. But I'll bring you back a video.'

James built Stuff an obstacle course among the breakfast dishes. 'I'd rather have Dad than a video,' he told the hamster. And that was when James had his good idea.

James made a tower of cereal bowls and put Stuff in the top one. Then he opened his dad's big important diary at Saturday.

With a red felt pen he wrote, '11 o'clock see James.' Stuff watched as James put the diary away.

'Will you come swimming with me today?' James asked his dad the next morning.

Mr Work-a-lot looked in his big important diary. 'Sorry, Son,' he said. 'I have to see James at 11 o'clock.'

At 11 o'clock Mr Work-a-lot found James playing paw-ball with Stuff. 'I've come to say sorry,' Mr Work-a-lot said, giving his son a hug.

'I love you,' James told his dad. And Stuff scored a goal.

Mr Work-a-lot and James went swimming – they're going to do it every week from now on.

God made people to live in families. And he wants parents and children to enjoy spending time together.

Dear Father in heaven,

help me to love my family. Please may I enjoy spending time with them and with you, my heavenly Father.

Amen.

'Be still, and know that I am God.'
Psalm 46:10

Jesus said, 'Come with me by yourselves
to a quiet place and get some rest.'
Mark 6:31

Collect the Little Lots Series
and answer these questions

Lucy Lie-a-lot

Where are the goldfish
called Round and About?

Harry Help-a-lot

What does Cheery Boy
the canary like to do?

Bobby Boast-a-lot

Is Champion the bravest
dog around?

Granny Grump-a-lot

How many mice has
Hunter the cat caught?

Lorna Look-a-lot

What interesting thing
has Sniff the dog found?

William Work-a-lot

How did Stuff the
hamster get his name?

Published by Christian Focus Publications,
Geanies House, Fearn, Tain, Ross-shire, IV20 1TW, Scotland.
www.christianfocus.com © Copyright 2005 Irene Howat Illustrated by Michel de Boer * Printed in the U.K.
The Little Lots series looks at positive and negative characteristics and values.
These titles will help children understand what God wants from our everyday lives. Other titles in this series include:
Lucy Lie-a-lot; Granny Grump-a-lot; Lorna Look-a-lot; Harry Help-a-lot; Bobby Boast-a-lot